HAPPY BDAY

To Ilyasson

Taylor Sun

Yes, Sir, it was Ol' Mrs. Buzzard who walked out of the end of that hollow log. FRONTISPIECE. *See page 54.*

CHILDREN'S THRIFT CLASSICS

The Adventures of Old Mr. Buzzard

THORNTON W. BURGESS

Illustrations by Harrison Cady

PUBLISHED IN ASSOCIATION WITH THE
THORNTON W. BURGESS MUSEUM AND THE
GREEN BRIAR NATURE CENTER,
SANDWICH, MASSACHUSETTS
BY
DOVER PUBLICATIONS, INC.
MINEOLA, NEW YORK

DOVER CHILDREN'S THRIFT CLASSICS

EDITOR OF THIS VOLUME: JANET BAINE KOPITO

Copyright

Bibliographical Note

The Adventures of Old Mr. Buzzard, first published by Dover Publications, Inc., in 2013 in association with the Thornton W. Burgess Museum and the Green Briar Nature Center, Sandwich, Massachusetts, who have provided a new introduction, is an unabridged republication of the work originally published as *The Adventures of Ol' Mistah Buzzard* by Little, Brown, and Company, Boston, in 1919.

International Standard Book Number

ISBN-13: 978-0-486-49726-6
ISBN-10: 0-486-49726-7

Manufactured in the United States by Courier Corporation
49726701
www.doverpublications.com

Introduction to the Dover Edition

The Adventures of Old Mr. Buzzard is a charming story in which Peter Cottontail learns some lessons from the new visitor to the "Green Forest." The book, originally known as *The Adventures of Ol' Mistah Buzzard,* finds Peter afraid at the beginning, convinced that the Buzzard must be some kind of hawk out to eat him, but eventually the two become friends. When Mr. Buzzard tells him things that Peter thinks could not possibly be true, the story takes a turn for the worse. By the end, Peter finds that seemingly simple questions can have surprising answers.

Thornton Burgess was America's preeminent author of children's nature stories from 1914 until 1962, when he wrote his last "Bedtime Story" for the *Herald Tribune* newspaper syndicate. During those years, he produced 70 books, 15,000 "Bedtime Story" episodes for the newspapers, and many stories for various magazines that remain uncounted. In each story, Burgess teaches us something about nature and includes at least one portrayal of a universal truth about human behavior.

In addition to his story writing, Thornton Burgess was an early and enthusiastic conservationist, honored for his work by the New York Zoological Society in 1919. Today, the Thornton Burgess Society seeks to continue his work and promote his goals by providing Nature Education for children both inside and outside of school. You can learn more about us at www.Thorntonburgess.org. We are gratified that Dover Publications recognizes the enduring quality of his work; every year they make more of his titles available to the general public at truly affordable prices. Their scholarship and attention to detail have been scrupulous. Together we hope to keep a personal awareness of nature part of a child's reality.

JOHN RICHMOND
The Thornton W. Burgess Society

Contents

Chapter   Page

I.   A Great Fear on the Green Meadows 1

II. Unc' Billy Meets an Old Friend 5

III. Ol' Mistah Buzzard Makes Friends. 8

IV. A Funny Dispute. 11

V.   Peter Grows Curious about
     Ol' Mistah Buzzard 15

VI. Peter Rabbit's Neck Aches 18

VII. The Result of Peter's Watching 21

VIII. Peter Rabbit is Jubilant. 24

IX. Peter Tells the Truth 27

X.   Ol' Mistah Buzzard Teases
     Peter Rabbit 30

XI. Peter is both Puzzled and Curious. 34

XII. Peter Consults Sammy Jay 37

XIII. Peter Arouses Sammy Jay's Interest 40

XIV. Sammy Jay Disappoints Peter 43

XV. Sammy Jay Gives Peter Directions. 47

XVI.   Peter Jumps Almost Out of His Skin. 50

XVII.   The Mystery is Cleared Up 53

XVIII. Ol' Mistah Buzzard Explains Things 56

XIX.   Sammy Jay Speaks His Mind. 59

XX.   Peter Asks a Personal Question 62

XXI.   Ol' Mistah Buzzard Starts a Story 65

XXII.   Ol' Mistah Buzzard Finishes His Tale. . . . 69

XXIII. Reddy Fox Runs for His Life 72

XXIV.   Peter Rabbit and Winsome
        Bluebird Gossip 75

XXV.   How Ol' Mistah Buzzard Warms
        His Toes 78

List of Illustrations

Yes, Sir, it was ol' Mrs. Buzzard who
    walked out of the end of that
    hollow log. *Frontispiece*

Unc' Billy pricked up his ears
    as he listened . . . . PAGE   3

"Do I know him! I should say I do!"
    exclaimed Digger the Badger . . . . . PAGE   12

"But—but—but—why, I thought you
    just said that you haven't any nest?"
    stammered Peter . . . . PAGE   31

"What?" cried Peter, jumping right up
    in the air . . . . PAGE   45

"'Ah tell you what, we-uns don't know
    how to build a nest.'" . . . . PAGE   67

The Adventures of
Old Mr. Buzzard

I

A Great Fear on the Green Meadows

IT had been a bad day on the Green Meadows. Yes, Sir, it had been a very bad day, especially for the littlest folks who live there. From the time jolly, round, red Mr. Sun first began his long climb up the blue, blue sky until it was almost time for him to go to bed behind the Purple Hills there had been great fear on the Green Meadows. And it was all because of a black speck way, way up in the sky, a black speck that kept going round and round and round and round in circles.

Danny Meadow Mouse poked his head out of his doorway and nearly twisted his head off as he watched the black speck go round and round. He shivered and ducked back into his house, only to stick his head out a few minutes later and do it all over again.

Peter Rabbit stuck to the dear Old Briar-patch all that day. He was perfectly safe there, but there wasn't any sweet-clover and he didn't dare go out on the Green Meadows to get any. By noon Peter's neck seemed ready to break from being twisted so much to watch that black speck in the sky.

And it was strangely still on the Green Meadows. The little birds forgot to sing. Mrs. Redwing kept

1

close hidden in the bulrushes on the edge of the Smiling Pool. Even Sammy Jay kept to the Green Forest. Only Blacky the Crow ventured out on the Green Meadows, but Blacky is so big that he is not much afraid of anything, and though once in a while he rolled an eye up at the black speck high in the sky, he went on about his business as usual.

Jimmy Skunk, who fears nothing and nobody, stopped to visit with Johnny Chuck. Johnny was sticking very close to his doorway that morning and every minute or two he rolled one eye up to see where the black speck was.

"I don't know what to make of it," said Johnny Chuck. "It isn't Old White-tail the Marsh Hawk, for he always flies close to the tops of the meadow grasses. It isn't fierce Mr. Goshawk, for he spends most of his time in the Green Forest. It isn't old King Eagle, for he never stays so long in one place. It isn't sharp-eyed old Roughleg, for he has gone back to his home in the Far North. And besides, none of them can fly round and round and round without flapping their wings as that fellow does. I wish he would go away."

But he didn't go away, only just kept sailing round and round over the Green Meadows and sometimes over the Green Forest. Every one was sure that it was a Hawk, and you know that most of the little meadow and forest folks are terribly afraid of Hawks, but no one could remember ever having seen such a wonderful flier among the Hawks. This big black

Unc' Billy pricked up his ears as he listened. *Page 4.*

fellow just sailed and sailed and sailed. Sometimes he shot down almost to the ground and then all the little meadow people scuttled out of sight. None was brave enough to stay and discover who the stranger was.

Now Unc' Billy Possum had been asleep all day and so he hadn't heard of the fright on the Green Meadows. It was just about the time that jolly, round, red Mr. Sun goes to bed when Unc' Billy came crawling out of his snug home in the hollow tree. Jimmy Skunk happened along just then. He had just seen the stranger glide down and settle for the night on a dead tree in the Green Forest, and he told Unc' Billy Possum all about it. Unc' Billy pricked up his ears as he listened. Then he grew very much excited.

"Ah reckons that that is mah ol' friend, Ol' Mistah Buzzard!" shouted Unc' Billy, as he started for the dead tree in the Green Forest.

II
Unc' Billy Meets an Old Friend

UNC' BILLY POSSUM lost no time in getting over to the dead tree in the Green Forest where Jimmy Skunk had seen the stranger go to roost for the night. Unc' Billy wanted to get there before the stranger had gone to sleep, for if it really were his old friend, Ol' Mistah Buzzard, as Unc' Billy felt sure it was, he had just got to say "howdy" that very night.

Now Unc' Billy is seldom caught napping, so though he was very sure that this was his old friend, he didn't intend to run any risk of furnishing a good supper for a hungry Hawk. So as Unc' Billy drew near the dead tree he crept up very quietly and carefully until he was where he could see the stranger clearly. There he sat on a branch of the dead tree. He was dressed in sooty black and he sat like an old man, his head drawn down and his shoulders hunched up. His head was bald and wrinkled.

Unc' Billy took one good look, and then he let out a whoop that made the stranger stretch out his long neck and begin to grin in pleased surprise.

"Hello, Ol' Mistah Buzzard! Where'd yo'all come from?" shouted Unc' Billy Possum.

"Ah reckon Ah done come straight from the sunny Souf, and Ah reckon this is the lonesomest land Ah ever done see. Ah'm going straight back where Ah come from. What yo'all staying up here fo' anyway, Unc' Billy?" said Ol' Mistah Buzzard.

Unc' Billy grinned. "Ah'm staying because Ah done like here mighty well, and Ah reckon that yo'all is going to like it mighty well, too," replied Unc' Billy.

Ol' Mistah Buzzard shook his head. "All day Ah done try to make friends, and every one done run away. Ah don' understand it, Unc' Billy. Ah cert'nly don't understand it at all." Ol' Mistah Buzzard shook his head sorrowfully.

Unc' Billy's wits are sharp, and he had guessed right away what the trouble was. So he explained to Ol' Mistah Buzzard how he had been mistaken for a fierce Hawk, and that the reason the Green Meadows had been so lonely was because all the little meadow people had been hiding and shivering with fear as they had watched Ol' Mistah Buzzard sailing round in the sky.

Pretty soon Mistah Buzzard began to see the joke. There he had been sailing round and round in the sky and growing lonesome for some one to talk to, and there down below him had been the very ones he wanted to make friends with, every one of them frightened most to death because they mistook him for a Hawk. Ol' Mistah Buzzard began to chuckle, and then he began to laugh.

"Ah reckon Ah'll have to stay a day or two just to see if yo'all is right," said he.

"Ah reckon yo'all will," replied Unc' Billy Possum. And Ol' Mistah Buzzard did.

III
Ol' Mistah Buzzard Makes Friends

UNC' BILLY POSSUM and Jimmy Skunk tramped through the Green Forest and over the Green Meadows till their feet ached. They had started out to visit the homes of all the little people who live there to tell them that the black stranger who had sailed the skies all the day before and frightened most of them so that they hardly dared put their noses outside of their own doors was as harmless as Peter Rabbit himself. You see they had all taken him for a fierce Hawk and had been frightened almost to death at the very sight of him. And all the time he wasn't a Hawk at all but just an old friend of Unc' Billy Possum, Ol' Mistah Buzzard, who had come up from way down South.

"My!" exclaimed Unc' Billy, as he stopped to mop his face because it was so warm, "Ah didn't know there were so many little people on the Green Meadows and in the Green Forest."

Just then he spied the Merry Little Breezes of Old Mother West Wind, and a happy thought came to him. He would get them to take his message around. Why hadn't he thought of it before? Of course the Merry Little Breezes were tickled to death, for they are always looking for something to do for others.

8

So off they raced as fast as they could, while Unc' Billy hurried back to have a chat with Ol' Mistah Buzzard.

At first many of the little meadow people were inclined to be very doubtful of the harmlessness of Ol' Mistah Buzzard. "How do you know?" demanded Danny Meadow Mouse of the Merry Little Breezes.

"Because Unc' Billy Possum has known him for a long time, and he says so," replied the Merry Little Breezes.

"I'll believe it when I see Unc' Billy risking his precious old skin where the stranger can reach him," said Danny, stretching his neck to try to see over the grass-tops.

The Merry Little Breezes clapped their hands joyously. "Look right down there by Farmer Brown's old hayrick," they cried.

Danny came out where he could see. Sure enough, there was Ol' Mistah Buzzard, large as life, sitting on the hayrick, and right down below him was sitting Unc' Billy Possum, and the two were talking and laughing fit to kill themselves. More than that, old Mrs. Possum was hurrying up with a broad grin, and behind her scampered all the little Possum children. When Danny saw that, he made up his mind that Ol' Mistah Buzzard really was harmless, and promptly started down to pay his respects.

One by one all day long the little meadow and forest people stole over to pay their respects to Ol' Mistah Buzzard. They found him all ready to make friends and so full of stories that most of them stayed to listen.

Late that afternoon when Ol' Mistah Buzzard sought the dead tree in the Green Forest to roost for the night, Unc' Billy Possum strolled by that way to see if his old friend was comfortable. Ol' Mistah Buzzard looked down at Unc' Billy, and his eyes twinkled.

"Ah reckon," said Ol' Mistah Buzzard, "that yo'all is right, and Ah sho'ly am going to stay here a right smart while. Ah sho'ly am."

IV
A Funny Dispute

"WHEN Ah left mah home way down Souf Ah cert'nly did hate to leave Brer Gopher and all the rest of mah friends," said Ol' Mistah Buzzard as he sat on his dead tree in the Green Forest.

"Did I hear you speak of Mr. Gopher?" asked Digger the Badger, who had come up just in time to hear the last words.

"Yo' sho'ly did, Brer Badger, yo' sho'ly did! Ah'm very fond of Brer Gopher," replied Ol' Mistah Buzzard. "Do yo' know him?"

"Do I know him! I should say I do!" exclaimed Digger the Badger, who, you know, came out of the Great West.

"Why, when I was a little fellow Mr. Gopher and I used to have digging matches, and he surely can dig! But I didn't know that he had moved down South."

"Why, what are you talking about, Brer Badger? He and his family have *always* lived down Souf!" exclaimed Ol' Mistah Buzzard.

Now Digger the Badger is quick-tempered. "You're wrong!" he shouted. "Mr. Gopher and his family have always lived out West!"

To tell any one that they are untruthful is a dreadful thing. Digger shouldn't have said that, even if he

11

"Do I know him! I should say I do!" exclaimed
Digger the Badger. *Page 11*.

did believe that Ol' Mistah Buzzard was telling an untruth. Ol' Mistah Buzzard was so taken aback that for a few minutes he couldn't find his tongue. When he did he talked very plainly to Digger the Badger. He called him names. The noise of the quarrel brought all the other little meadow and forest people on the run to see what it all meant.

"Ah tell yo' Brer Gopher and his family have always lived in the Souf, and Ah don' believe yo' know Brer Gopher at all!" said Ol' Mistah Buzzard.

Digger the Badger fairly danced up and down, he was so mad. "Not know him!" he shrieked. "Not know him! Why I know every hair in his coat!"

Ol' Mistah Buzzard stared at Digger a full minute. "What was that yo' said?" he asked slowly.

"I said I know every hair in Mr. Gopher's coat," snapped Digger.

Ol' Mistah Buzzard looked around the circle of little meadow and forest people in triumph. "Ah knew he didn't know Brer Gopher," said he. "Brer Gopher's coat isn't made of hair at all; it's of shell."

It was Digger's turn to stare. Then he began to laugh. He laughed and laughed and laughed. "Shell!" he gasped. "Shell!" Then he went off into another fit of laughter, while Ol' Mistah Buzzard grew very red and angry.

"What's all this fuss about?" demanded Old Mother West Wind, who was on her way home to the Purple Hills.

When she had heard all about it she began to laugh. "You are both right and both wrong," said she. "Mr. Gopher who lives way down South does wear a shell coat, and he is cousin to Spotty the Turtle, but lives on the land and digs holes in the ground. Mr. Gopher whom Digger the Badger knows does wear a coat of hair, and he is a distant relative of Striped Chipmunk. And the two Mr. Gophers are not related at all. Now make up."

And Ol' Mistah Buzzard and Digger the Badger did.

V

Peter Grows Curious about Ol' Mistah Buzzard

The more we have the more we want;
   At least I find that true
With almost every one I know;
   Pray, is it so with you?

PETER RABBIT, who had been calling at the Smiling Pool, had learned so many curious and interesting things about Spotty the Turtle and Grandfather Frog that his head almost ached as he started for the Green Forest one morning in the spring after Ol' Mistah Buzzard's first appearance. You would think that Peter's curiosity ought to have been satisfied for once, but it wasn't. You see, curiosity is one of those things that is seldom really satisfied.

As Peter hopped along, lipperty-lipperty-lip, he looked up to see that Redtail the Hawk was not near enough to be dangerous. There was no sign of Redtail, but high up in the blue, blue sky, sailing round and round, was Ol' Mistah Buzzard. Now ever since Ol' Mistah Buzzard had come up the first time from way down in Ol' Virginny to make his home in the Green Forest for the summer, Peter had been greatly interested in him. In the first place no one else could sail and sail and sail without moving his wings as could Ol' Mistah Buzzard. In the second place Ol' Mistah Buzzard was the only one whom Peter was acquainted with who had a bald head. King Eagle is called bald-headed, but isn't bald at all. On the other hand Ol' Mistah Buzzard, who isn't a Buzzard at all but a Vulture, hasn't a feather on his head. He had told the story of how his family first became bald-headed, and ever since then Peter had taken the liveliest interest in Ol' Mistah Buzzard.

This spring Ol' Mistah Buzzard had brought Mrs. Buzzard up from Ol' Virginny with him, and Peter had spent many hours watching them sail round and round high up in the blue, blue sky, so high sometimes that they were little more than specks. This morning as he watched Ol' Mistah Buzzard, it suddenly popped into Peter's head that he hadn't seen Mrs. Buzzard for some time. Ol' Mistah Buzzard was alone now, and he had been alone every time Peter had seen him of late, only Peter hadn't happened to think of it before.

Peter paused and gazed up at Ol' Mistah Buzzard thoughtfully. "I wonder," said he, thinking aloud as he sometimes does, "if anything can have happened to Ol' Mrs. Buzzard, or if she has grown tired of the Green Forest and gone back to her old home." He wrinkled his forehead in a way he has when he is puzzled or trying to think. Then as a thought popped into his head his face cleared.

"I know!" he exclaimed. "It must be that Mrs. Buzzard is keeping house. Of course. Why didn't I think of that before? All my feathered friends, and some who are not my friends, have nests now, so why shouldn't Mistah and Mrs. Buzzard have a nest? They have. I feel it in my bones. They've got a nest somewhere, and Mrs. Buzzard is taking care of the eggs, and that is why I haven't seen her lately. Now I wonder where that nest is. I should like to see it. I believe I'll have a look around in the Green Forest. Such big folks as Ol' Mistah and Mrs. Buzzard must have a big nest, and it ought not to be hard to find it."

Fairly bubbling over with curiosity Peter started to run again towards the Green Forest.

VI

Peter Rabbit's Neck Aches

Who blindly seeks will seldom find
The thing he has upon his mind.

IF he does it will be by accident. It will be pure luck. Peter Rabbit should have known this. He had tried it often enough. But Peter is a heedless, happy-go-lucky fellow, and I guess he always will be. So when he made up his mind that he would like to see the nest of Ol' Mistah and Mrs. Buzzard, he promptly started to look for it without having the least idea where to look or what to look for.

He thought he had an idea, but Peter always thinks he has an idea. The trouble is he never thinks enough to know whether or not he has an idea. If Ol' Mistah Buzzard had a nest, of course it must be in the Green Forest, reasoned Peter. And because all the big birds of his acquaintance built big nests high up in the trees, of course Ol' Mistah Buzzard must do the same thing. That was as far as Peter went in his thinking.

"All I need to do is to keep my eyes wide open for a new big nest in a tall tree, and that ought to be easy enough to find," thought Peter, as he scampered into the Green Forest, lipperty-lipperty-lip.

Once in the Green Forest he no longer hurried. It is hard work to hurry with your head tipped back so as to see the tops of the trees. Presently Peter's neck began to ache. He sat down under a friendly little hemlock-tree to rest his aching neck. When it felt better he went on again, his head tipped back as before. Whenever he saw a bundle of sticks or leaves high up in a tree he was sure that he had found Ol' Mistah Buzzard's nest. Then he would sit down and stare at it very hard and presently would discover that it was an old nest of Redtail the Hawk or of Blacky the Crow or of Chatterer the Red Squirrel or his cousin, Happy Jack the Gray Squirrel. Then he would work his head back and forth to get the kink out of his neck, sigh, and start on again.

"My goodness! I didn't suppose there were so many old nests in the Green Forest," muttered Peter as for the twentieth time he was disappointed. "And what an everlasting lot of trees! Why the Green Forest is all trees!"

Then Peter looked all around to see if anybody had overheard that foolish remark. Nobody had, and Peter grinned at his own foolishness. He rubbed his neck and started on, head tipped back as before. At last he could stand it no longer.

"I've got to give it up for now, anyway," said he ruefully. "My neck aches so that I can't stand it any longer." Of course he meant the ache, not his neck. "I want awfully to find that nest of Ol' Mistah Buzzard's, but I guess I'll have to wait until another day.

I didn't realize that the Green Forest is so big. Why at this rate it will take me all the rest of the summer and more too to look in every tree. If I only had some idea just what part of the Green Forest to look in, it would help some."

Right then and there a sudden idea popped into his funny little head, and he grinned sheepishly. "Why didn't I think of it before?" he said right out loud. "I'll just watch Ol' Mistah Buzzard and see where he goes when he comes down from up in the blue, blue sky. He'll be sure to come down near his nest, and then all I'll have to do is to go right over there and find it. My gracious, goodness me, but my neck certainly does ache! I think I'll rest a bit and try my new plan later."

And Peter did this very thing.

VII
The Result of Peter's Watching

THE result of Peter Rabbit's foolish search for the nest of Ol' Mistah Buzzard was a stiff and aching neck from tipping his head back so long in order to look up in the trees. The next day, however, the ache was gone, but his curiosity was not; it was greater than ever. So Peter scampered, lipperty-lipperty-lip, over to the edge of the Green Forest to try his new plan of watching Ol' Mistah Buzzard.

"It can't fail," thought Peter. "No, Sir, it can't fail. All I have to do is to be patient. Ol' Mistah Buzzard is bound to visit his nest, and if I watch him why of course I'll find out where that nest is. Anyway, I'll find the locality, and then it will be easy enough to find the nest because such a great big fellow as Ol' Mistah Buzzard must have a great big nest, and a great big nest cannot very well be hidden."

So Peter made himself comfortable in a little tangle of briars on the edge of the Green Forest where he could look up in the blue, blue sky and watch Ol' Mistah Buzzard sailing round and round. Now as everybody knows, Ol' Mistah Buzzard spends much of his time doing this very thing. He will sail about for hours because for him it is just about as easy as sitting still, and at the same time it gives him a chance to see all that is going on below, for Ol' Mistah Buzzard's eyes are very, very keen. At first it was easy for Peter to sit there and do nothing but watch Ol' Mistah Buzzard, for Peter is very fond of sitting still and doing nothing. Watching Ol' Mistah Buzzard really amounted to doing nothing.

But after awhile Peter found that staring up in the sky that way made him sleepy. In spite of all he could do his eyelids would close for a minute or two at a time. Then they would fly open and he would look up hastily to find Ol' Mistah Buzzard still a speck high up in the blue, blue sky. More and more often Peter's eyes closed for tiny naps, and though he didn't know it those naps grew longer and longer. At last his eyes flew open to see nothing but the blue, blue sky and a few fleecy white clouds. Of Ol' Mistah Buzzard there was no sign.

Peter rubbed his eyes and looked again this way and that way, but it was all too evident that Ol' Mistah Buzzard was no longer sailing round and round high up in the blue, blue sky. He had come down while Peter was taking a nap. Peter almost cried with vexation. But there was no one to blame but himself. He knew that. If he had kept his eyes open he would have seen Ol' Mistah Buzzard come down. But he hadn't, and so he was no wiser than before.

Peter called himself names. Yes, Sir, he did just that very thing. He was so provoked with himself that he actually called himself names. "Anyway, it is quite useless to sit here any longer," he concluded. "I'll have to try again later in the day or to-morrow."

So Peter started for home in the dear Old Briar-patch. Half way there he glanced up from force of habit. Up in the blue, blue sky some one was swinging round and round in great circles. Peter stopped short and stared. Then he grinned. It was Ol' Mrs. Buzzard this time. She must have come out of the Green Forest while Peter was on his way home. If he had sat still a little longer he would have seen her rise into the air, and would have known just where she had come from. Peter turned and scurried back to his hiding-place.

"This time I won't go to sleep!" he declared. "I'll keep my eyes on Ol' Mrs. Buzzard if I have to stick brambles into me to keep awake. I have an idea that she won't stay up as long as Ol' Mistah Buzzard, anyway."

VIII
Peter Rabbit is Jubilant

TO be jubilant is to be filled with joy and gladness. This was exactly Peter Rabbit's condition. He was so jubilant that he had to kick up his heels half a dozen times. You see, Ol' Mrs. Buzzard had stayed up in the air only a very short time. In fact, Peter had been in his hiding-place on the edge of the Green Forest only a very short time when she came down from high up in the blue, blue sky. He hadn't had time to get sleepy this time.

Down, down, down she came and disappeared among the tree-tops. But Peter had seen just where she had disappeared. It was very near a certain tall pine-tree. He knew that he could go straight to that certain tall pine-tree without any trouble. And once there he had no doubt at all that he would find that nest. A nest big enough for such a big bird as Ol' Mrs. Buzzard surely couldn't be hidden so that he couldn't find it.

So Peter was jubilant and hopped and skipped happily on his way toward that certain tall pine-tree. Forgotten was his stiff neck of the day before. Forgotten was his disappointment that very morning when Ol' Mistah Buzzard, whom he had been watching, had come down out of the blue, blue sky

24

while Peter was napping. His curiosity was about to be satisfied. He was about to find the nest of Ol' Mistah and Mrs. Buzzard. Not a single doubt entered his foolish little head. In fact, he counted that nest as good as found already.

So he hopped and he skipped, and he skipped and he hopped on his way to the certain tall pine-tree, and all the way he thought what a smart chap he was.

"Of course," said Peter to himself, "Ol' Mistah and Mrs. Buzzard think their nest is a secret that no one will find out, and yet they give that secret away to any one as smart as I am. I don't suppose it ever has entered their heads that any one would watch them. Of course when I have found that nest I won't tell anybody. That wouldn't be fair."

It didn't enter Peter's head that he himself wasn't fair in spying and trying to find that nest. Of course, it was no business of his. Certainly not. But Peter didn't once think of this. Curiosity had taken possession of him, and when curiosity takes possession of anybody they are likely to give little heed to right and wrong.

So all in good time Peter came to the certain tall pine-tree near which he had seen Ol' Mrs. Buzzard disappear among the tree tops. First he looked that over carefully, though he didn't expect to find the nest in it because it was such a conspicuous tree. Con-spic-u-ous means to stand out from surrounding things so as to be easily seen. Peter didn't think that Ol' Mistah and Mrs. Buzzard would build their nest in a tree that would be so easily and quickly picked out from among the other trees, but he looked it over carefully to make sure. While he was doing this a voice startled him.

"Good mo'ning, Brer Rabbit. Yo' seem to be looking fo' something. Can Ah help yo' find it?" said the voice.

Peter whirled about to find Ol' Mistah Buzzard looking down at him from the top of a tall dead tree which is a favorite roost of his, and in his eyes was a twinkle. Peter was confused. Yes, Sir, Peter was very much confused. He didn't know just what to say.

IX
Peter Tells the Truth

Remember this: 'Tis always well
The truth and nothing else to tell.

PETER RABBIT didn't know what to say when Ol'
Mistah Buzzard asked him what he was looking for and if he could help find it. No, Sir, Peter
didn't know what to say. He was quite confused.
In the first place he had forgotten that Ol' Mistah
Buzzard's favorite roost was a tall dead tree close
by, and he hadn't seen Ol' Mistah Buzzard until the
latter spoke. This had startled him, but what had
confused him still more was the fact that he didn't
quite see how he could answer Ol' Mistah Buzzard's
questions.

However, Peter is truthful. He has found that not
only is it wrong to tell an untruth, but that in the end
it never pays. So now he blurted out the truth.

"I—I—I," he stammered and stopped. Ol' Mistah
Buzzard's eyes twinkled, but he said nothing, and in
a minute Peter began again. "I was just sort of wondering if you and Mrs. Buzzard have a nest up in that
tall pine-tree," said he.

"Then Ah'll just save yo' the trouble of wondering any mo'," replied Ol' Mistah Buzzard, his eyes

twinkling more than ever. "We-uns haven't. What is mo', we-uns wouldn't dream of building a nest in a tree like that—a tree that is so much taller and bigger than the rest that all who come this way are just naturally bound to look at it. May Ah ask, Brer Rabbit, what fo' yo' seem so interested in mah nest?"

Peter hung his head. Of course, there was no reason except idle curiosity, and he was ashamed to admit that. But he did. Yes, Sir, he did. He is too truthful not to admit his own faults.

"I just thought I would like to see it, Mistah Buzzard," he replied. "It just popped into my head the other day that probably you and Mrs. Buzzard have a nest, and I got to wondering what it is like. I've seen the nests of Blacky the Crow and Redtail the Hawk and Hooty the Owl and of a good many others, and I got to wondering if you build a nest anything like those I have seen. So being over this way, I thought I would just call around. Of course I don't mean the least bit of harm by it."

"Ah see," replied Ol' Mistah Buzzard. "May Ah ask yo', Brer Rabbit, how it happened that yo' thought that mah nest might be over here?"

"Why, I saw Ol' Mrs. Buzzard disappear among the tree-tops right near here," said Peter eagerly.

"Which Ah take it means that yo' were watching her to see where she went," returned Ol' Mistah Buzzard drily.

"Y-e-s," confessed Peter, and looked very much ashamed of himself. You see, he knew then that Ol'

Mistah Buzzard knew that he had been spying, and spying is something that nobody likes.

"But yo' didn't see just where she did go, did yo'?" continued Ol' Mistah Buzzard.

"No," replied Peter. "I thought that if I knew somewhere near the spot where your nest is I could find it. Such big folks as you and Mrs. Buzzard must have a big nest. You do, don't you, Mr. Buzzard?"

"Hm-m-m, Ah don' see it anywhere," said Ol' Mistah Buzzard, looking this way and that. All the time his eyes twinkled more than ever. "What makes yo' so sure Ah have got a nest, Brer Rabbit?"

X
Ol' Mistah Buzzard Teases Peter Rabbit

OL' MISTAH BUZZARD looked down at Peter Rabbit and chuckled as he waited for Peter's reply to his question. It was a noiseless chuckle, so of course Peter didn't hear it. Peter scratched his long left ear with his long right hind foot. Then he scratched his long right ear with his long left hind foot. Finally he made reply.

"Of course, I don't know for sure that you have a nest," said he, "but I think you must have. All the birds I know have nests this time of year. Besides, this year you brought Mrs. Buzzard up from the South with you, and I've noticed that lately I haven't seen her very often. She doesn't sail round and round way up in the blue, blue sky with you the way she did when she first arrived. So I think she must be taking care of her eggs. And if you have eggs to be taken care of, why of course you must have a nest. I—I wish you would tell me where it is, Mistah Buzzard. I'd just love to see it, and I will promise not to tell a single living soul where it is." Peter was very much in earnest.

"Not even Mrs. Peter?" asked Ol' Mistah Buzzard.

Peter hesitated. You know he usually tells Mrs. Peter everything. He doesn't believe in keeping

"But—but—but—why I thought you just said that
you haven't any nest?" stammered Peter. *Page 32*.

secrets from Mrs. Peter. But this was different from most secrets, and he did so want to see that nest. So at last he agreed that he wouldn't tell anybody, not even Mrs. Peter.

Ol' Mistah Buzzard leaned down with a great pretense of secrecy. "Ah'm going to tell yo' something, Brer Rabbit," said he, and Peter's long ears stood straight up expectantly. "Ah haven't any nest. No, Suh, Ah haven't any nest," he concluded.

Peter looked the disappointment he felt. He had been so sure that now he was to find out what he had so wanted to know. "But—but what is the reason that Mrs. Buzzard keeps out of sight so much?" he asked.

"That," whispered Ol' Mistah Buzzard, as if afraid he might be overheard, "is the real secret. She is so busy with household cares that she hasn't time for anything else."

"But—but—but—why I thought you just said that you haven't any nest?" stammered Peter, looking quite as puzzled as he felt. In fact, he looked so puzzled that Ol' Mistah Buzzard had to turn away his head to hide a grin.

"That is just what Ah did say," replied Ol' Mistah Buzzard. "That is just what Ah did say. We-uns haven't any nest."

"Then how can Mrs. Buzzard be so busy with household cares?" demanded Peter. His voice was just a little sharp. He was beginning to suspect that

Ol' Mistah Buzzard was trying to have fun at his expense.

"She is sitting on our two aiggs, and one of these days Ah reckon we-uns are going to have two of the finest babies in the Green Forest," asserted Ol' Mistah Buzzard.

"But you just said you haven't any nest!" exclaimed Peter.

"So Ah did! So Ah did!" replied Ol' Mistah Buzzard. "Cert'nly Ah did. We-uns haven't any nest."

XI
Peter is both Puzzled and Curious

"MISTAH BUZZARD, you are making fun of me! That's what you are doing—making fun of me!" exclaimed Peter Rabbit indignantly.

"Ah'm doing nothing of the kind, Brer Rabbit," declared Ol' Mistah Buzzard. "What fo' do you say that?" He looked very solemn, though if the truth be known he was having hard work to keep a twinkle of mischief from showing in his eyes.

"Because," replied Peter in a tone that showed that he felt hurt and decidedly put out, "you tell me that you and Mrs. Buzzard haven't any nest, and then you tell me that Mrs. Buzzard is so busy with household cares that she hasn't time to fly in the blue, blue sky as she did when she first arrived. You tell me that you haven't any nest, and then you tell me that you have two eggs. Your story doesn't hang together. It doesn't hang together at all. No, Sir, it doesn't hang together at all. If you have two eggs, of course you have a nest. If you haven't a nest, why how can you have two eggs? Tell me that! I can believe one half your story, but only half. Do you know which half I believe?"

Ol' Mistah Buzzard turned his head as if to look off over the Green Forest, but really to hide a grin.

34

When he looked down at Peter again he appeared to
be indignant in his turn.

"Ah'm not used to having mah word doubted, Brer
Rabbit," said he with dignity. "Ah always have had
a most friendly feeling fo' yo', Brer Rabbit, but Ah
reckons Ah don' want anything mo' to do with one
who tells me to mah face that he doesn't believe
what Ah say. No, Suh, Ah reckon Ah don' want anything mo' to do with any such person as that."

Ol' Mistah Buzzard shifted his position awkwardly
and turned his back on Peter Rabbit.

Peter didn't know what to do. He and Ol' Mistah
Buzzard had been the best of friends, and he didn't
want that friendship to end. He had been quite honest in saying that he didn't believe that story. He
didn't believe it because he couldn't believe it. At
least, he didn't see how he could. But now that Ol'
Mistah Buzzard seemed to be actually offended, a
little doubt crept into Peter's head. He had lived
long enough to know that there are some things very
hard to believe which are true nevertheless.

For some time he sat staring at Ol' Mistah Buzzard's back, and while he stared he did a lot of thinking. Finally he decided that Ol' Mistah Buzzard's
friendship was worth a great deal more than satisfy-
ing his own idle curiosity.

"Mistah Buzzard," said he in a timid small voice,
"of course, if you say on your honor that you are not
joking me and that you really have two eggs and no
nest I'll believe you. I wouldn't for the world have

you think that I doubt your word of honor. I wouldn't think of doing such a thing. You see, I never heard of such a thing as anybody having eggs and no place to put them, and so of course I thought you were joking. I'm sorry if I've offended you. Won't you tell me where those eggs are?"

Ol' Mistah Buzzard kept still so long that Peter feared that after all he was too much offended to make up. But at last he turned around and looked down at Peter.

"Brer Rabbit," said he, "Ah accept your apology. Ah have seen so many things hard to believe mahself that Ah know how yo' feel. What Ah told yo' is true on mah honor. We-uns haven't any nest, but Mrs. Buzzard and Ah done got two as fine aiggs as ever yo' have seen. Where they are is the secret of we-uns. All Ah can tell yo' is that they are here or hereabouts. Ah reckon that now Ah'll stretch my wings a bit."

With this Ol' Mistah Buzzard spread his great wings, flapped them a few times and then sailed up, up, up in the blue, blue sky, leaving Peter more puzzled and curious than ever.

XII
Peter Consults Sammy Jay

PETER RABBIT stared up in the blue, blue sky, watching Ol' Mistah Buzzard sail round and round as only Ol' Mistah Buzzard can. Peter sighed. It was clear to him that he had learned all he could learn from Ol' Mistah Buzzard about those eggs which the latter said Ol' Mrs. Buzzard was caring for.

"He said that they are here or hereabouts, and yet not in a nest," said Peter to himself. "What he means by that is too much for me. If they are here, I ought to be able to find them. At least, I ought to be able to find Mrs. Buzzard, and of course if I find her, I will find those eggs. It seems simple enough."

Peter looked this way and looked that way, but mostly up in the trees. Somehow he couldn't, he just couldn't believe that Mrs. Buzzard could be anywhere else. But for all his looking he found nothing, and at last he gave up. The puzzle was too much for him. He was just about to start for his home in the dear Old Briar-patch when he heard the voice of Sammy Jay not far off.

"What I can't find perhaps Sammy can," thought Peter. "There are mighty few things Sammy Jay can't find out if he sets out to. Perhaps he knows all about

37

those eggs of Ol' Mistah Buzzard's now. Anyway, it won't do any harm to ask him."

So off Peter started to look for Sammy Jay. It didn't take him long to find Sammy, for the latter's blue coat is easy to see when he is flying about. "Sammy Jay," began Peter, as soon as he was near enough, "did you ever hear of anybody having eggs and no nest to put them in?"

"Certainly," replied Sammy promptly.

"Who?" demanded Peter eagerly.

"Boomer the Nighthawk, for one," replied Sammy.

"What?" cried Peter as if he hadn't understood, or at least as if he thought he hadn't understood. There was astonishment in the very tone of his voice.

"Doesn't Boomer have a nest? If he doesn't, where does Mrs. Boomer lay her eggs?"

"Where would she lay them, Mr. Curiosity?" retorted Sammy. "She lays them on the ground, or on a flat rock. Mrs. Whip-poor-will does the same thing. I supposed everybody knew that. Where have you been—asleep?"

"No," retorted Peter shortly, for it rather upset him to learn that he hadn't known these facts about two of his familiar friends. "But I'm not interested in Boomer and Whip-poor-will just now. It is some one else I want to know about."

"All right," replied Sammy. "What have you got on your mind? The sooner you get it off the better. You are looking too excited, Peter. You know too much excitement is bad for your health."

Sammy Jay was teasing, and Peter knew it. He made up a wry face at Sammy, a good-natured face, you know. Then he laughed as he replied:

"Sammy Jay, tell me, do you know where Mrs. Buzzard lays her eggs?"

Sammy scratched his topknot thoughtfully. "I can't say that I do," he replied. Then, noticing how disappointed Peter looked, he hastened to add: "But I guess I can find out if I want to. Why do you want to know?"

XIII
Peter Arouses Sammy Jay's Interest

WHEN Sammy Jay asked Peter Rabbit why he was so anxious to know where Ol' Mrs. Buzzard had laid her eggs, Peter hesitated. Then he blurted out the whole story. He told Sammy how it had popped into his head that he never had seen the nest of Ol' Mistah and Mrs. Buzzard; how he had made up his mind that of course they must have a nest; how he had thought that such big people must have a big nest; how he had looked for it until his neck ached; how he had watched Ol' Mrs. Buzzard, and finally how Ol' Mistah Buzzard had told him that they hadn't a nest but that they had two eggs.

"If they have two eggs, where are they? I ask you that, Sammy Jay?" concluded Peter.

Sammy had listened with growing interest. It so happens that he never had given a thought to the affairs of Ol' Mistah and Mrs. Buzzard, which was rather odd, as Sammy is usually interested in the affairs of everybody in his neighborhood. Again he scratched his topknot thoughtfully.

"I shall have to look into this," said he at last, winking at Peter. "If Ol' Mistah Buzzard told you on his word of honor that he hasn't a nest, why, he hasn't, and that is all there is to that. If he hasn't a nest and yet Mrs. Buzzard is sitting on two eggs, why those two eggs must be somewhere."

Peter nodded. "Of course," said he.

"And if others who have no nests lay their eggs on the ground, why shouldn't Mrs. Buzzard?" continued Sammy. "Why shouldn't she do as Mrs. Boomer the Nighthawk and Mrs. Whip-poor-will do?"

"True enough," said Peter gravely. "True enough. Why shouldn't she? I hadn't thought of that because, you see, I didn't know about Mrs. Boomer and Mrs. Whip-poor-will until you told me. Of course, those eggs must be on the ground. The question is, where? I haven't seen Ol' Mrs. Buzzard anywhere on the ground. I wish I had thought of the ground before. If I had it would have saved my neck. Funny, isn't it, that any one so fond of the air and flying so high should lay eggs on the ground?"

"We don't know yet that they are on the ground," Sammy Jay broke in. "You are jumping at things just as usual, Peter Rabbit. Now I am going to see what I can find out. If my eyes are not sharp enough to find any one as big as Mrs. Buzzard, I shall think there is something the matter with them." Sammy spread his wings ready to fly.

"If you find out where those eggs are, you'll come back and tell me, won't you, Sammy?" Peter asked anxiously.

"Perhaps," replied Sammy Jay, with a grin.

"Oh, but you must!" cried Peter. "You wouldn't have known anything about them if I hadn't told you."

"I don't know anything about them now," retorted Sammy. "That is why I am going to look for them."

"But please, Sammy, come back and tell me if you find them," begged Peter. "I'll wait right here."

"Perhaps," replied Sammy provokingly, and flew away.

XIV
Sammy Jay Disappoints Peter

When once you've got your mind all set
　　Upon some special thing
How dreadful disappointing 'tis
　　To have your hopes take wing.

SOMEHOW Peter Rabbit felt in his bones that Sammy Jay would find out what he himself hadn't been able to find out, for all his trying—Ol' Mistah Buzzard's secret. Perhaps it was because Sammy is a famous hand at finding out the secrets of others. Perhaps it was because Peter has tried in vain to keep secrets of his own from Sammy. Anyway, as he waited there in the Green Forest for Sammy to return, it was with a feeling that when he did come back he surely would have the secret about the eggs of Ol' Mistah and Mrs. Buzzard.

It was a long time before he saw or heard anything of Sammy, but at last he heard his harsh voice in the distance, and presently he caught sight of his blue coat among the trees. Peter fairly danced with impatience. He just couldn't sit still. It seemed to him as if Sammy were taking an unusually long time. He stopped in almost every tree. Finally Peter ran to meet him.

"Well, did you find those eggs?" cried Peter as soon as he was near enough.

Sammy Jay looked very much dejected and disappointed. "No," said he, "I didn't find those eggs."

Peter looked at Sammy Jay sharply to make sure that he was telling the truth, for sometimes, I am sorry to say, Sammy doesn't tell the truth. But this time Sammy looked so honest that Peter didn't doubt him. He tried not to let his disappointment show, but he couldn't help it. "I—I thought surely you'd find them," said he. "I guess if you couldn't nobody can."

That pleased Sammy Jay, and he flew down a little nearer to Peter. "I'm going to tell you something, Peter," said he. "I didn't find those eggs because there aren't any."

"What?" cried Peter, jumping right up in the air.

"It's a fact," replied Sammy. "Ol' Mistah Buzzard and Mrs. Buzzard haven't any eggs. I know it."

"How do you know it?" demanded Peter. "Ol' Mistah Buzzard told me on his honor that they had two."

"And Ol' Mrs. Buzzard told me on her honor that they haven't any," replied Sammy. "What is more, I believe her."

Peter stared at Sammy Jay with such a funny look on his face that Sammy had to turn his head to hide a smile.

"So you found Mrs. Buzzard," said Peter, when he could find his voice. "Did she tell you that they haven't any nest?"

"What?" cried Peter, jumping right up in the air. *Page 44*.

"I didn't ask her," replied Sammy. "All I asked about was the eggs, and as I have already told you they haven't any."

"How do you know that she told the truth?" asked Peter suspiciously.

"I know because I know," retorted Sammy, which wasn't much of an answer.

"Well," said Peter at last, "I think I'll give up and go home to the dear Old Briar-patch. Of course those eggs were no business of mine, anyway. It's funny to me, though, that Ol' Mistah Buzzard should tell me that they have two, and Mrs. Buzzard should tell you that they haven't any. I don't understand it at all."

"By the way, Peter," said Sammy, as Peter started for home, "I saw something which will interest you and perhaps make up for your disappointment."

Peter pricked up his ears hopefully. "What was it?" he demanded.

XV
Sammy Jay Gives Peter Directions

PETER RABBIT was all curiosity as he demanded what it was that Sammy Jay had found that would be of interest to him. Of course, Sammy had known that he would be. It doesn't take much to arouse Peter's curiosity. Some people are just that way. A word or two is enough to get them all worked up. Sammy cocked his head to one side and looked at Peter shrewdly.

"Do you think that you can follow my directions exactly?" he asked.

Peter nodded his head vigorously. "Of course," he replied. "Just give them to me and see. But what is it you saw that you think will interest me? It might not, you know."

"I don't know anything of the sort," replied Sammy. "On the contrary, I know that it *will* interest you. It interested me a great deal, and anything that will interest me is bound to interest you. But I'm not going to tell you what it is. I'm going to let you have the fun of finding it. If when you find it you don't say that it is one of the most surprising things you have seen in all your life, my name isn't Sammy Jay."

By this time Peter was all ears, as the saying is. He had forgotten all about his disappointment over

47

his failure to find the secret of Ol' Mistah and Mrs. Buzzard. He was impatient to be off in quest of this mysterious and interesting thing which Sammy Jay had found.

"All right, Sammy; I'll wait to find out for myself what it is," said he. "It is fun sometimes not to know just what it is you are looking for. Where did you say this thing is?"

"I didn't say," replied Sammy, his sharp eyes twinkling with mischief. "First you must promise to do exactly as I say."

"I promise," declared Peter with great promptness.

"Very good," said Sammy. "The first thing to do is to go over to that dead tree where you saw Ol' Mistah Buzzard this morning. You know where that is, don't you?"

"Of course I know where that is," retorted Peter.

"When you get there, turn to your right until you come to a little thicket of young hemlock-trees," continued Sammy. "Back of that thicket is a great big hollow log."

"I know all about that log," Peter interrupted. "I've hidden in it more than once. What next?"

"When you reach that log you must be very quiet," replied Sammy. "You must steal along beside it to the open end without making a sound. You mustn't rustle so much as a leaf."

"My, this sounds exciting!" cried Peter. "What then?"

"Poke your head around and look inside. You'll see what it is that I found," replied Sammy.

A sudden suspicion crept into Peter's head. "There isn't anything there that is likely to hurt me, is there?" he demanded. "Reddy Fox isn't asleep in there, or anything like that?"

"No," replied Sammy Jay. "There isn't anybody or anything there to hurt you. But there is something there to interest you."

Sammy looked so earnest that Peter's suspicions left him at once. In fact, he was a little ashamed of having been suspicious.

"All right," said he, "I'm off." And away he went, lipperty-lipperty-lip.

XVI
Peter Jumps Almost Out of His Skin

PETER RABBIT'S curiosity was so aroused by what Sammy Jay had told him that he scampered through the Green Forest as fast as he could make his legs go, and that is very fast indeed. Lipperty-lipperty-lip, lipperty-lipperty-lip, lipperty-lipperty-lip scampered Peter, and didn't once look behind. If he had he might have seen Sammy Jay following, though it is doubtful, for Sammy was taking great care to keep out of sight.

But Peter didn't look behind. His thoughts were all on that mysterious and interesting thing that he was to find in the big hollow log behind the thicket of young hemlock-trees. When he reached the tall dead tree on which Ol' Mistah Buzzard delights to sit, he glanced up. Ol' Mistah Buzzard wasn't there, and Peter kept on without a pause. Presently he came to the thicket of young hemlock-trees and quickly slipped through this.

Right on the other side lay the great hollow log. As soon as he reached this Peter stopped running. Mindful of what Sammy Jay had said, he crept forward on tiptoe as it were, taking the greatest care not to make a sound. He even held his breath. He put his feet down so as not to snap a single dry twig or rustle a single dry leaf. It was very exciting. It was the most exciting thing Peter had done for a long time. Every step or two he stopped to listen. Not a sound was to be heard, not even the sighing of the pine-trees, for there wasn't even one of the Merry Little Breezes about to make them sigh. It was a lonely spot, a very lonely spot. The very silence made the mystery all the greater.

Little by little Peter crept along beside the great hollow log. It was one of the biggest logs in all the Green Forest. On many a stormy winter night it had sheltered him. He knew all about that old log, inside and out. At least, he thought he did. Now as he reached the end of it he stopped. He was eager to peep around and look inside, yet somehow he dreaded to. Just why he didn't know. Probably it was because Sammy Jay had made such a mystery of what was inside. You know how all of us are apt to be a little afraid of things that are mysterious.

Half a dozen times Peter started to peep around, and each time he drew back. At last he mustered up his courage. His curiosity overcame all his fears. Sammy Jay had said that there was nothing in there to harm him, and if that was the case, it was foolish to be so timid. So Peter poked his head around the end of the old log, his eyes very big with wonder and anticipation. Before he could really see what was inside there came a sharp, angry hiss almost in his very face. It was one of the loudest hisses Peter ever had heard.

Poor Peter! He was so frightened that he jumped nearly out of his skin. In fact he turned two back somersaults and then without waiting to see who had frightened him so, away he went, lipperty-lipperty-lip, until he was quite out of breath. Then a sound reached him that made him pause. It was very like the voice of Sammy Jay laughing.

XVII
The Mystery is Cleared Up

AT the sound of Sammy Jay's voice Peter Rabbit stopped running. In fact, he stopped altogether. He sat up and listened. Yes, there was no doubt about it, that was the voice of Sammy Jay, and it came from right near that great hollow log where Peter had just received such a fright. Moreover, Sammy was chuckling as if at a great joke. Peter looked back, and in his eyes a suspicion grew and grew.

"Sammy Jay knew I was going to get that fright, and he followed me to see what would happen. He played a joke on me, that's what he did," declared Peter indignantly. "But who was it in that old log that could hiss like that? That's what I want to know. Sammy told me that nothing would harm me and somehow I believe him. I suppose I'm foolish to, after such a trick, but just the same I don't believe Sammy would send me into real danger. I don't know any one who could hiss like that except one of the Snake family, and I'm too big for any of them to hurt me, excepting Buzztail the Rattler or Copperhead, and somehow I don't believe it was either of them. I think I'll go back and find out who it was."

So Peter turned back and very, very carefully he approached the great hollow log. He found a place where he could see the open end of the great hollow log and be unseen himself, for he was hidden in a clump of ferns. At first he couldn't make out anything, for it was dark inside that old log. Then little by little he made out a dim shape inside, but whose shape it was he couldn't for the life of him tell. Presently he discovered Sammy Jay in a tree just above the old log. Sammy was talking to some one. After a little the dim shape in the hollow log moved and then out came—can you guess who? The very last person in the world Peter Rabbit expected to see— Ol' Mrs. Buzzard!

Yes, Sir, it was Ol' Mrs. Buzzard who walked out of the end of that hollow log, and when he saw her Peter was just as much surprised as when that terrible hiss had frightened him. He couldn't possibly have been any more surprised. Of course, he had nothing to fear from Ol' Mrs. Buzzard, so he promptly walked out of his hiding-place.

"Was it you that hissed when I looked in the hollow log a few minutes ago?" he demanded.

"It cert'nly was," replied Mrs. Buzzard. "Yo' startled me so Ah didn't rightly know who you were, so Ah hissed. Mah goodness, but yo' cert'nly can run, Brer Rabbit!"

Peter grinned but he let it pass, for his curiosity was all in what Mrs. Buzzard was doing in that old log. "If you please, Mrs. Buzzard, what were you doing in that old log?" he asked politely.

"That's mah home fo' a while," replied Mrs. Buzzard proudly.

"What?" cried Peter, as if he didn't trust his own ears.

He hopped a few steps nearer and peeped in. Then his eyes grew wide with astonishment. There was no nest there, but there were two little white downy birds. "Why—why—why—" stammered Peter and then stopped.

Sammy Jay laughed right out. "You see," said Sammy, "Ol' Mistah Buzzard told the truth when he said that they had no nest. Also he told the truth when he said that they had two eggs. That is, he thought he told the truth. He didn't know that they had hatched. And Ol' Mrs. Buzzard told the truth when she told me that they hadn't any eggs. And I told the truth when I said that there was something here to interest you and that wouldn't hurt you. So the great mystery is cleared up, and I hope your curiosity is satisfied, Peter Rabbit."

"It is," declared Peter, drawing a long breath.

XVIII
Ol' Mistah Buzzard Explains Things

WHEN Peter Rabbit said that his curiosity was satisfied he really meant it. He had found out what he so wanted to know. He had found out where Mrs. Buzzard had laid her eggs. He had found out that it was true that Ol' Mistah and Mrs. Buzzard do not build a nest. He had found out that in this particular case the eggs had been laid in a great hollow log. So for the time being his curiosity was satisfied.

He promised Ol' Mrs. Buzzard that he would keep her secret. He laughed with her and with Sammy Jay at the way he had been frightened when Ol' Mrs. Buzzard had hissed right in his face, and then he bade them farewell and started for home in the dear Old Briar-patch. Of course he was full of the strange discovery about the ways of Ol' Mistah and Mrs. Buzzard and could think of nothing else.

"It certainly is queer that such big birds shouldn't have a nest," thought Peter, as he sat chewing a leaf of sweet clover. "I never would have thought of looking in a hollow log for their home, never in the world. I wonder what they would do if there wasn't a hollow log big enough. Hollow logs like that one are not to be found everywhere."

This thought was enough to awaken Peter's ever-ready curiosity once more. As he thought it over and wondered, his curiosity grew. So the next day he scampered back to the Green Forest and headed straight for the tall dead tree where Ol' Mistah Buzzard delights to sit. Ol' Mistah Buzzard was there, and his eyes twinkled as he saw Peter coming.

"I know your secret now, Mistah Buzzard," cried Peter, as soon as he reached the foot of the tree.

"Then Ah hopes yo'll keep it," replied Ol' Mistah Buzzard gravely.

"I will," promised Peter. "But Mistah Buzzard, there is one thing more I want to know."

"Only one thing? Yo' surprise me, Brer Rabbit," replied Ol' Mistah Buzzard.

Peter grinned, for he knew that Ol' Mistah Buzzard was joking him about his curiosity. "There is only one thing now," said he, "but there may be more things later."

"Well," replied Ol' Mistah Buzzard, "what is that one thing? Get it off your mind, and perhaps Ah can help yo' out."

"It is this: What do you and Mrs. Buzzard do for a place for your eggs when there isn't a big hollow log handy?" Peter replied promptly.

"Why, that's simple, ve'y simple indeed, Brer Rabbit," said Ol' Mistah Buzzard. "Mrs. Buzzard just naturally lays her aiggs on top of a big stump if there happens to be one handy. If there isn't she just lays her aiggs on the ground. Yo' know, Brer Rabbit, the ground is always handy."

Ol' Mistah Buzzard looked down and grinned, and Peter grinned back. "Do you mean that she doesn't put any grass or sticks or anything under them?" asked Peter.

Ol' Mistah Buzzard nodded. "Of course," said he, "she picks out a place where she reckons she isn't going to be disturbed. Ol' Mrs. Buzzard is a little bit peevish when she done be sitting on her aiggs. She don' like to be disturbed. So she picks out a place where she can be quite by herself, lays her aiggs and then takes care of them until they hatch, and that is all there is to it."

XIX
Sammy Jay Speaks His Mind

THE more Peter Rabbit thought it over, the stranger it seemed to him that such big people as Ol' Mistah Buzzard and Mrs. Buzzard should be content to have no nest. If he hadn't seen with his own eyes those two Buzzard babies in the great hollow log, and if he hadn't heard with his own ears Ol' Mistah Buzzard say that when there was no big hollow log handy Mrs. Buzzard would lay her eggs on top of a stump, and when there was no stump handy she would lay them on the bare ground, he wouldn't, he was sure, have been able to believe that anything of the kind could be true.

There was no one with whom he could talk the matter over save Sammy Jay. You see Peter had promised not to give the Buzzard secret away, and Sammy was the only one Peter knew of who also knew that secret. So the first chance he got Peter asked Sammy what he thought of the matter, and if he supposed there was any good reason why the Buzzards didn't build a nest.

"Shiftlessness!" replied Sammy scornfully. "Just plain shiftlessness. They are too lazy and shiftless to go to the trouble of building a nest, that's all. Ol' Mistah Buzzard is just naturally lazy, and Mrs. Buzzard

59

is just like him. Have you ever seen Ol' Mistah Buzzard do a stroke of work since you've known him?"

Peter couldn't remember that he had and said so.

"Of course you haven't," asserted Sammy in the same scornful voice as before. "Of course you haven't. Why? Because he hasn't done any work. All he does is just sail round and round in the blue, blue sky or sit in the sun on that old dead tree. When he's sailing round and round he doesn't move his wings any more than he has to. He doesn't even catch his own food."

"I don't hold that against him," declared Peter promptly, thinking how he had always to be on the watch to escape Hooty the Owl and the members of the Hawk family, "but now you mention the matter, I wonder what he does eat. I hadn't thought of it before. Do you know what he does eat?"

"Yes," replied Sammy, "I know." There was both scorn and disgust in his voice this time. "He eats things that no one else would think of eating. He eats dead things, and he don't seem to care how long they have been dead. He is the most shiftless fellow I know of. You are rather shiftless yourself, Peter, but compared with Ol' Mistah Buzzard you are almost industrious. I can't understand how any one can be so shiftless and lazy. It doesn't surprise me any to find out that he and Mrs. Buzzard don't build a nest. I guess I would have been more surprised to find that they did. I know a good many shiftless folks, but none equal to Ol' Mistah Buzzard and Mrs. Buzzard. Sometimes I wonder if the reason they have bald heads is because they are too lazy to grow feathers on them."

Sammy grinned at his own joke, and Peter laughed. "You certainly have got a mighty small opinion of the Buzzard family, Sammy," said he.

"I certainly have," retorted Sammy. "I may have faults, but laziness isn't one of them. The idea of great big able-bodied birds like Mistah and Mrs. Buzzard being content to have their eggs on the ground without so much as a stick or a straw under them! I call it a disgrace to the whole feathered tribe."

Sammy Jay flirted his tail, tossed his head, and then flew away, leaving Peter to think things over and, I suspect, with a lot less respect for Ol' Mistah Buzzard than he had had before.

XX
Peter Asks a Personal Question

To be too personal is impolite,
So watch your tongue and guide it right.

TO ask personal questions means to ask questions about things which really concern only those to whom you may happen to put the questions. Personal matters are those which are the business of no one but the ones whom they immediately concern, and there is no greater rudeness or impoliteness than to ask about them out of idle curiosity. Peter Rabbit knows this. Anyway, he should know it. He ought to have learned it by this time. But Peter's curiosity is forever leading him to do things which he shouldn't do.

The more Peter thought over what Sammy Jay had said about the laziness and shiftlessness of Ol' Mistah and Mrs. Buzzard, the more he was inclined to think that Sammy must be right about the matter. It certainly seemed as if no one as big and strong as Ol' Mistah Buzzard would be content to do without a nest of some sort unless he were indeed very lazy and shiftless. Peter himself is not at all fond of work, you know, and right down in his heart he had a little feeling of sympathy for Ol' Mistah Buzzard in avoiding unnecessary work. But even Peter felt that it was quite unpardonable that Ol' Mistah Buzzard's children should have no nest at all. The more he thought about it, the more it seemed impossible that any one could be quite so shiftless as this. His respect for Ol' Mistah Buzzard had received a great shock. At last he made up his mind that he would find out if what Sammy Jay had said could be true.

So over to the Green Forest scampered Peter, lipperty-lipperty-lip, straight to the tall dead tree where Ol' Mistah Buzzard delighted to sit when he was not sailing round and round high up in the blue, blue sky.

Ol' Mistah Buzzard was there holding his wings half spread for the air to blow through them and the sun to fall on them. His eyes twinkled as he saw Peter.

"Yo' seem to have something on your mind, Brer Rabbit. What is it this time?" said he.

Peter hesitated a minute as if a little ashamed. Then he blurted out what he had on his mind. "Are you really and truly shiftless, Mistah Buzzard?" he asked.

Ol' Mistah Buzzard closed his wings and blinked his eyes very rapidly as if he didn't quite know what to think.

"What's that, Brer Rabbit?" he demanded sharply. "Ah think Ah couldn't have understood yo'. What's that yo' said?"

"I asked if you are really and truly shiftless," repeated Peter.

Ol' Mistah Buzzard ruffled up all his feathers indignantly. "Ah reckons yo' done lost all your manners, Brer Rabbit," said he. "That's a mighty personal question. Who say Ah'm shiftless? Who say that? Ah want to know who say Ah'm shiftless?"

Ol' Mistah Buzzard looked so fierce that Peter began to be afraid of him and wished with all his might that he had held his tongue.

"I—I—" he began, then hesitated. Then he hurried on. "You know, Mistah Buzzard, you haven't any nest and—and I've heard it said that it is because you and Mrs. Buzzard are too lazy and shiftless to build one. I thought there might be some other reason, and so I came to you to find out," he finished lamely.

XXI
Ol' Mistah Buzzard Starts a Story

DO you wonder that Ol' Mistah Buzzard was indignant when Peter Rabbit blurted out such a personal question? At first Ol' Mistah Buzzard was tempted to speak his mind very plainly to Peter and tell him just what he thought of people who gossip about others and their personal affairs, but Peter looked so innocent of any intention to meddle and so truly puzzled that Ol' Mistah Buzzard promptly recovered his good nature.

"Mah affairs are really no business of yours, Brer Rabbit, and Ah reckons yo' know it, but just to set your mind at rest, Ah'm going to tell yo' a story," said he.

At this Peter pricked up his ears and settled himself contentedly. He had heard Ol' Mistah Buzzard tell stories before, and he knew that a story from him was bound to be interesting, whether it was true or not.

"Ah'm not saying that this is the true reason why my family doesn't build nests," began Ol' Mistah Buzzard with a twinkle in his eyes, "but it is a story that has done been handed down to we-uns from way back at the beginning of things when the world was young. It was in the days when Granny and

Granddaddy Buzzard, the first of mah family, lived, and eve'ybody was learning or trying to learn how to live. Yo' see, in those days nobody knew just what was best to do. Eve'ybody was trying to work out fo' himself what was best, and learning something every day. Of course, eve'ybody made mistakes, lots of them, Granddaddy and Granny Buzzard just like the rest, and it was because of one of these mistakes that they didn't have a nest like the rest of the birds.

"Yo' see, when the first nesting season came around and Ol' Mother Nature passed the word along fo' all the birds to prepare places fo' their aiggs and young, there were most as many ideas as there were kinds of birds. Each pair had their own idea of what a nest should be made of and where it should be put, and fo' a while there was a right smart lot of confusion. Yes, Suh, there was a right smart lot of confusion.

"Ol' Granddaddy and Granny Buzzard were naturally easy-going. It was powerful warm down there where they lived, and Ah reckons it looked to them plumb foolish to do any mo' work than they had to. Ah know it looks that way to me. Building nests was new to eve'ybody, and nobody knew the best way of going about it.

"'Ah tell you what,' say Granddaddy Buzzard to Granny Buzzard, 'we-uns don't know how to build a nest. Eve'ybody else has got a different idea, and Ah reckons we-uns haven't any idea at all. Ah don' see any sense in getting all heated up and tired out

"'Ah tell you what, we-uns don't know
how to build a nest.'" *Page 66.*

trying to do something when we-uns don' know what it is we want, so Ah reckons we-uns will just sit tight and watch our neighbors. When they done got their nests built we-uns will just go around and see which one we like best and which is easiest to build, and then we'll build one like it.' This suited Ol' Granny Buzzard and she wasn't a mite slow in saying so.

"Excuse me, Brer Rabbit. Here come Mrs. Buzzard and Ah reckons she wants to see me about something particular. If yo' will wait here Ah will finish mah story when Ah comes back."

With this off flew Ol' Mistah Buzzard, leaving Peter to wait as patiently as he could for the end of the story.

XXII
Ol' Mistah Buzzard Finishes His Tale

IT seemed to Peter Rabbit that Ol' Mistah Buzzard was gone a long time. You know how it is when you are waiting for the end of a story when the story-teller has been called away. Really it was only a few minutes that Ol' Mistah Buzzard was gone, but it seemed to Peter ages and ages.

"Let me see, where was Ah?" said Ol' Mistah Buzzard as soon as he had once more seated himself comfortably on the tall dead tree under which Peter sat.

"You had reached the place where Granddaddy and Granny Buzzard decided to wait to see how the other birds built their nests," prompted Peter.

"Just so. Just so," replied Ol' Mistah Buzzard. "Well Granddaddy and Granny Buzzard just sat around and watched the other birds and said nothing, and looked wise. Ah reckons there was a terrible time building those first nests, and when they were all done Ah reckons none of them was much as nests go now. There was a right smart lot of fussing and worrying and quarreling, but Granddaddy and Granny Buzzard kept out of it and when any one asked them where they were building their nest and what they were making it of, they simply looked wise as befo' and said nothing.

"Of course eve'ybody tried to make a powerful secret of where their nests were, but sitting around just watching, Granddaddy and Granny Buzzard found out where most of them were. They waited until the last of their neighbors had finished their nests and then they just went around looking at each to see how it was made and what it was made of. They found all kinds of nests, some made of sticks and some made of straw, and some made of mud, and some made of moss. Seemed like nary one of them just suited Granddaddy and Granny Buzzard. Anyway, they kept hoping that they would see one that would suit better, and so they kept a-looking and a-looking and a-looking. Granny Buzzard wanted her nest made out of something soft and comfortable, and Granddaddy Buzzard wanted it made of something it wouldn't be much work to find and less work to put together.

"So they couldn't make up their minds, and time went drifting along and drifting along, and first thing they knew eve'y last one of the other birds had a nest and aiggs, and here was Granddaddy and Granny Buzzard without even a place picked to build a nest. When Granddaddy Buzzard realized this he scratched his haid and began to look worried. Granny Buzzard scratched her haid and looked mo' worried.

"'Pears like to me we-uns haven't got time to build a nest,' said Granddaddy Buzzard at last.

"'Ah was thinking that ve'y same thing,' replied Granny Buzzard. 'If we stop to build a nest now, we-uns will be so late the season's gwine to be all over befo' we know it. Ah reckons Ah ought to be sitting on those aiggs right now.'

"'Ah reckons that's right,' replied Granddaddy Buzzard, 'but fo' the life of me, Ah don' see what we-uns gwine to do about it.'

"Two or three days later Granny Buzzard called him to one side in a place where nobody is likely to come along and showed him two aiggs right on the ground. 'Ah reckons that is better than any nest,' said she. 'Nobody's gwine to look on the ground fo' aiggs, and if they do there's a powerful lot of ground to look over for two aiggs. The wind can't blow them out of a nest, and when they hatch the babies can't fall and hurt themselves. Ah'm gwine to sit right here until they hatch. Ah reckons this nest building is all plumb foolishness anyway.'

"'Ah reckons it is too,' replied Granddaddy Buzzard with a sigh of relief because he hadn't got to help build a nest.

"And ever since then the Buzzard family done get along without nests and have saved theirselves a powerful lot of work," concluded Ol' Mistah Buzzard.

And to this day Peter isn't sure whether the Buzzards are smart or just shiftless.

XXIII
Reddy Fox Runs for His Life

IT was only a few days after Peter Rabbit found out the secret of Ol' Mistah and Mrs. Buzzard that Reddy Fox took it into his head to visit that part of the Green Forest where lay the great hollow log in which were the two helpless Buzzard babies. Reddy wasn't looking for them. He had no interest in Ol' Mistah Buzzard or his affairs. Probably if he ever had thought of the matter at all he would have taken it for granted, as Peter had, that Ol' Mistah Buzzard's nest would be in a tall tree.

The fact is he was hunting for the nest of Mrs. Grouse and it had popped into his head that it might be over in that particular part of the Green Forest. He knew all about that big hollow log. There are few such places Reddy doesn't know about. Many a time had he peeped into it, hoping to surprise Peter Rabbit there.

Just as Peter did Reddy stole softly alongside the old log and poked his head around the end to look inside. Just imagine how surprised he was when two funny little heads were suddenly raised and two funny mouths opened wide. The baby Buzzards had heard him and thought it was their mother coming to feed them.

Reddy jumped in front of the opening and sat down to stare, for he never had seen any babies at all like these and he didn't know what to make of them. "Now whose babies are these?" he muttered. "Not that it makes any real difference, for they will make just as good a dinner as if I knew all about them," he added and grinned as only Reddy can. Then he started to crawl in after them.

Right that very instant things began to happen. With an angry hiss such as Reddy never had heard before something struck him and knocked him over and over. Before he could get his breath or even look to see what or who had hit him he received such a shower of blows that it seemed to him there wasn't a spot on his whole body that wasn't hit. The air seemed to be filled with great claws and beaks which tore his red coat and made him yell. He had just one thought and that was to get away from that place, to get as far away from it as he could.

At last he managed to get to his feet and then how Reddy did run! He didn't even look behind to see who it was who had pounded and scratched and pecked him so. He simply ran and ran and ran, whimpering with every breath. He was running for his life. At least he thought he was. Every instant he expected to be knocked over again.

Of course you know what had happened. Mrs. Buzzard had been standing just back of a little tree only a few steps from the great hollow log. She had seen Reddy just as he started to crawl in after her precious babies and she hadn't wasted any time. She had rushed at him like a fury. With her great wings she had pounded him and with claws and beak she had pulled his hair out and torn his coat. And all the time she had kept up a hissing quite frightful to hear.

When Reddy at last got away from her she had not tried to follow him, but had rushed back to her precious babies to make sure that they were safe. Reddy didn't know this. He was too badly scared to know much of anything save that he wanted to get home as quickly as his legs could take him. He was sure this terrible creature was right at his heels all the way there, and to this day he doesn't know whose babies he found, for it was a long, long time before he dared visit that part of the Green Forest again and by that time the baby Buzzards were big enough to sail round and round high up in the blue, blue sky like their father, Ol' Mistah Buzzard.

XXIV
Peter Rabbit and Winsome Bluebird Gossip

TO gossip is to talk about other people and what they are doing, or what they have done, or what they are going to do. Peter Rabbit and Winsome Bluebird were gossiping in the dear Old Briar-patch. Winsome sat in a little cherry-tree, and right under him sat Peter. Winsome had just arrived from way down South to spread the glad news that Mistress Spring was on her way and would soon reach the Green Meadows, the Green Forest and the Smiling Pool. You see, Winsome is the herald of Mistress Spring and keeps just a little way ahead of her. When the little meadow and forest people first see his beautiful blue coat, or hear his soft sweet whistle, they know that Mistress Spring is surely on the way and not very far behind, and then great joy fills their hearts. First comes gentle Sister South Wind to prepare the way, then Winsome Bluebird, and after him beautiful Mistress Spring.

Peter Rabbit was brimful of curiosity, just as he always is. You see, it was a long time since he had last seen Winsome Bluebird and all the other birds who had gone to the far-away South when the leaves began to drop in the fall, and of course he wanted to know all about his old friends and neighbors, how they were, what they had been doing, and when they were coming back.

And Winsome wanted to know all about how Peter and Reddy Fox and all the other little people who hadn't gone to the beautiful South had spent the long winter. So there was a great deal to talk about. Yes, indeed, there was a very great deal to talk about. Winsome felt that he ought to be flying about over the Green Meadows and the Green Forest where other little people could see him and hear him and so know that he had arrived, but he had traveled a very, very great distance and he was tired, and so he sat and rested, and while he rested he gossiped with Peter Rabbit.

"Is Ol' Mistah Buzzard on his way here?" asked Peter eagerly.

"Not yet," replied Winsome. "He won't start until after he is sure that Mistress Spring has got here," replied Winsome.

Peter looked a little disappointed, for there is nothing that he enjoys more than to watch Ol' Mistah Buzzard sail round and round, way, way up in the blue, blue sky. He is rather fond of Ol' Mistah Buzzard, is Peter, for big as he is Mistah Buzzard never offers to hurt any of the very little people, not even little Danny Meadow Mouse. "Why isn't he starting right away?" he asked.

"Well, you see," replied Winsome, "Mistah Buzzard doesn't like the cold."

"But it isn't cold now!" interrupted Peter. "Why, this isn't cold at all. You ought to have been here when it really was cold—when the Smiling Pool and the Laughing Brook were covered with ice, and the Green Meadows and the Green Forest were all white with snow, and poor Mrs. Grouse was a prisoner under the hard icy crust. Then it *was* cold! Why, this isn't cold at all."

Winsome Bluebird ruffled up his feathers just a little. It was almost like a shiver. "This is cold enough for me!" said he. "Tell me about poor Mrs. Grouse, Peter. Did she get out?"

"You tell me about Ol' Mistah Buzzard first, and how he spends the winter, and then I'll tell you about poor Mrs. Grouse," replied Peter.

"All right," said Winsome. "There isn't a great deal to tell, but I'll do the best I can. I'll tell you how he warms his toes."

XXV
How Ol' Mistah Buzzard Warms His Toes

OFTEN and often had Peter wondered how Ol' Mistah Buzzard and all his other feathered friends who had flown away to the far-away South at the first hint that Jack Frost was on his way to the Green Meadows spent the long winter. It seemed to Peter that the South must be a very wonderful and very strange place. He was not at all sure that he would like it. It must be very nice not to have to worry about finding enough to eat, and yet—well, Peter did have lots of fun in the snow. It seemed to him that all those little people who went away certainly missed a great deal. Now Winsome Bluebird had returned from that far-away South with the good news that Mistress Spring was not far behind, and Winsome had promised to tell him all the news of Ol' Mistah Buzzard and the other friends, and how Ol' Mistah Buzzard keeps his toes warm.

"You see," began Winsome, "Ol' Mistah Buzzard was born and brought up in the South where it is always warm, and he just can't stand cold weather. No, Sir, he can't stand cold weather. Why, weather that you and I would call comfortable will make him shiver and shake. That is why he wasn't ready to come up with me. Now I come ahead of Mistress

Spring, but Ol' Mistah Buzzard won't start until he is sure that Mistress Spring has been here some time and he will be sure not to have cold feet."

"Cold feet!" cried Peter. "Who ever heard of such a thing! Why I run around on the snow and ice all winter long, and I never have cold feet."

"Well, Ol' Mistah Buzzard has them," replied Winsome Bluebird. "Yes, Sir, he is always complaining about cold feet. You know he hasn't any shoes or stockings like you, Peter, so between his bare feet and his bald head he has, or thinks he has, a great deal to worry about every time there is a cool day, and they sometimes have cool days even way down South. Then you will always find Ol' Mistah Buzzard warming his toes."

Peter scratched his head in a funny way. "If you please, Winsome, how does he warm his toes?" asked Peter. "I never see him warming his toes when he is up here. He's always sailing round and round way up in the blue, blue sky or else sitting on a dead tree in the Green Forest. I've never heard him complaining of cold feet or seen him try to warm his toes."

"Of course you haven't!" replied Winsome. "He doesn't have cold feet then because it's summer time. It's just as you say, if you don't see him up in the blue, blue sky you are sure to find him on that old dead tree. But down South it is different. If you want to see him there and he isn't way up in the blue, blue sky trying to get nearer to Mr. Sun so as to warm his bald head, why you just look for him on a toe-warmer."

Peter's eyes seemed to fairly pop out with curiosity. "What's a toe-warmer?" he demanded. "I never heard of such a thing. What does it look like?"

Winsome Bluebird chuckled softly. "Have you ever been up by Farmer Brown's house?" he asked.

Peter nodded.

"Then you've seen that thing on the roof out of which smoke sometimes comes," continued Winsome.

Again Peter nodded.

"Well," continued Winsome, "if Farmer Brown's house was down South, that thing out of which the smoke comes would be one of Ol' Mistah Buzzard's toe-warmers."

Peter looked sharply at Winsome to see if he really meant what he said. "Doesn't anybody live in those houses down South?" he asked suspiciously.

"Of course," replied Winsome. "If they didn't how could Mistah Buzzard warm his toes?"

"And he isn't afraid?" persisted Peter, as if it was very hard to believe.

"Afraid!" cried Winsome. "Why, he hasn't anything to be afraid of. Mr. Buzzard is thought a great deal of, a very great deal of, in the South, and no one would hurt him for the world. So every house has a toe-warmer for him, which is very nice for him. And you won't see him back here until it is so warm that he forgets all about cold feet," concluded Winsome Bluebird.

And so we will leave Peter Rabbit watching for the return of Ol' Mistah Buzzard, and we will leave Ol' Mistah Buzzard warming his toes on a chimney-top, for this is the end of this little book.

THE END